Homing Pigeon

Kelly Doudna

Illustrated by Neena Chawla

Consulting Editor, Diane Craig, M.A./Reading Specialist

ABDO
Publishing Company

Published by ABDO Publishing Company, 4940 Viking Drive, Edina, Minnesota 55435.

Printed in the United States.

Credits
Edited by: Pam Price
Curriculum Coordinator: Nancy Tuminelly
Cover and Interior Design and Production: Mighty Media
Photo Credits: Corbis Images, ShutterStock

Library of Congress Cataloging-in-Publication Data

Doudna, Kelly, 1963-
    Homing Pigeon / Kelly Doudna; illustrated by Neena Chawla.
        p. cm. -- (Fact & fiction. Critter chronicles)
    Summary: Pidge Pigeon, a cadet in military school, is given an important task as his last test of skill before graduation. Alternating pages provide facts about pigeons.
    ISBN 10 1-59928-440-5 (hardcover)
    ISBN 10 1-59928-441-3 (paperback)

    ISBN 13 978-1-59928-440-8 (hardcover)
    ISBN 13 978-1-59928-441-5 (paperback)
    [1. Delivery of goods--Fiction. 2. Military cadets--Fiction. 3. Homing pigeons--Fiction. 4. Pigeons--Fiction]
I. Chawla, Neena, ill. II. Title. III. Series.

    PZ7.D74425Hom 2006
    [E]--dc22

                                                                                        2006005538

SandCastle Level: Fluent

SandCastle™ books are created by a professional team of educators, reading specialists, and content developers around five essential components—phonemic awareness, phonics, vocabulary, text comprehension, and fluency—to assist young readers as they develop reading skills and strategies and increase their general knowledge. All books are written, reviewed, and leveled for guided reading, early reading intervention, and Accelerated Reader® programs for use in shared, guided, and independent reading and writing activities to support a balanced approach to literacy instruction. The SandCastle™ series has four levels that correspond to early literacy development. The levels help teachers and parents select appropriate books for young readers.

Emerging Readers   **Beginning Readers**   **Transitional Readers**   **Fluent Readers**
(no flags)   (1 flag)   (2 flags)   (3 flags)

These levels are meant only as a guide. All levels are subject to change.

FACT & FiCTION

This series provides early fluent readers the opportunity to develop reading comprehension strategies and increase fluency. These books are appropriate for guided, shared, and independent reading.

FACT The left-hand pages incorporate realistic photographs to enhance readers' understanding of informational text.

FiCTION The right-hand pages engage readers with an entertaining, narrative story that is supported by whimsical illustrations.

The Fact and Fiction pages can be read separately to improve comprehension through questioning, predicting, making inferences, and summarizing. They can also be read side-by-side, in spreads, which encourages students to explore and examine different writing styles.

FACT OR FiCTION? This fun quiz helps reinforce students' understanding of what is real and not real.

SPEED READ The text-only version of each section includes word-count rulers for fluency practice and assessment.

GLOSSARY Higher-level vocabulary and concepts are defined in the glossary.

SandCastle™ would like to hear from you.

Tell us your stories about reading this book. What was your favorite page? Was there something hard that you needed help with? Share the ups and downs of learning to read. To get posted on the ABDO Publishing Company Web site, send us an e-mail at:

sandcastle@abdopublishing.com

Pigeons have a very strong homing instinct. They can find their way back to their home roosts from hundreds of miles away.

Pidge Pigeon is a cadet in military school. He is training to carry important messages between commanding officers.

Because pigeons are so good at navigating, they have been used to carry messages since ancient times.

Pidge's teacher, Commander Cooper, says, "Cadet, as a last test of your skill, I want you to deliver the invitations for next week's graduation ceremony."

Homing pigeons can fly as far as 600 miles in one day.

Pidge gives Commander
Cooper a big salute. "Yes, sir!"
he exclaims. Pidge slings the bag
full of invitations over his shoulder. He puts
on his goggles and sets off on his mission.

Most birds drink by taking sips of water and tipping their heads back. Pigeons use their beaks like straws and suck up a steady flow of water.

Pidge reads the address on the first invitation, 100 Roost Road. "I know where that is," Pidge thinks to himself. "This will be easy." He sips his energy drink and heads for Roost Road.

11

Experts believe that pigeons use Earth's magnetic field as well as landmarks to navigate.

Pidge delivers the first few invitations with no trouble. But then the sky clouds over, and it becomes stormy. A strong gust of wind blows Pidge around until he no longer knows which direction he's supposed to go.

13

Pigeons have excellent eyesight. In addition to seeing all colors that humans can see, pigeons see other colors that people can't see.

Pidge waits in a tree until
the next morning. The sun is bright,
and he spies the city hall clock tower in
the distance. "Whew!" he sighs with relief.
"Now I know which way to go."

Homing pigeons can reach speeds over 50 miles per hour when they fly.

Fiction

Within an hour, Pidge delivers the last invitation. He races home to the academy. "Mission accomplished, Commander Cooper!" he says proudly. Commander Cooper says, "Well done, Cadet!"

17

A pigeon will stay with the same mate throughout its adult life. Both parents help care for their young.

The next week, at the graduation ceremony, Pidge spots his parents in the crowd on the ledge. "We're proud of you, son!" they coo. They clap their wings as Pidge crosses the stage and receives his diploma.

FACT OR FICTION?

Read each statement below. Then decide whether it's from the FACT section or the FICTION section!

  1. Pigeons go to military school.

  2. Pigeons can read.

  3. Pigeons can see colors that humans can't see.

  4. Pigeons can fly over 50 miles per hour.

ANSWERS
1. fiction 2. fiction 3. fact 4. fact

Pigeons have a very strong homing instinct. They | 8
can find their way back to their home roosts from | 18
hundreds of miles away. | 22

Because pigeons are so good at navigating, they | 30
have been used to carry messages since ancient times. | 39

Homing pigeons can fly as far as 600 miles in one | 50
day. | 51

Most birds drink by taking sips of water and tipping | 61
their heads back. Pigeons use their beaks like straws | 70
and suck up a steady flow of water. | 78

Experts believe that pigeons use Earth's magnetic | 85
field as well as landmarks to navigate. | 92

Pigeons have excellent eyesight. In addition to | 99
seeing all colors that humans can see, pigeons see | 108
other colors that people can't see. | 114

Homing pigeons can reach speeds over 50 miles per | 123
hour when they fly. | 127

A pigeon will stay with the same mate throughout | 136
its adult life. Both parents help care for their young. | 146

21

Pidge Pigeon is a cadet in military school. He $\quad$ 9
is training to carry important messages between $\quad$ 16
commanding officers. $\quad$ 18

Pidge's teacher, Commander Cooper, says, $\quad$ 23
"Cadet, as a last test of your skill, I want you to $\quad$ 35
deliver the invitations for next week's graduation $\quad$ 42
ceremony." $\quad$ 43

Pidge gives Commander Cooper a big salute. $\quad$ 50
"Yes, sir!" he exclaims. Pidge slings the bag full of $\quad$ 60
invitations over his shoulder. He puts on his $\quad$ 68
goggles and sets off on his mission. $\quad$ 75

Pidge reads the address on the first invitation, $\quad$ 83
100 Roost Road. "I know where that is," Pidge $\quad$ 92
thinks to himself. "This will be easy." He sips his $\quad$ 102
energy drink and heads for Roost Road. $\quad$ 109

Pidge delivers the first few invitations with no $\quad$ 117
trouble. But then the sky clouds over, and it $\quad$ 126
becomes stormy. A strong gust of wind blows $\quad$ 134

Pidge around until he no longer knows which direction he's supposed to go.

Pidge waits in a tree until the next morning. The sun is bright, and he spies the city hall clock tower in the distance. "Whew!" he sighs with relief. "Now I know which way to go."

Within an hour, Pidge delivers the last invitation. He races home to the academy. "Mission accomplished, Commander Cooper!" he says proudly. Commander Cooper says, "Well done, Cadet!"

The next week, at the graduation ceremony, Pidge spots his parents in the crowd on the ledge. "We're proud of you, son!" they coo. They clap their wings as Pidge crosses the stage and receives his diploma.

GLOSSARY

academy. a school that teaches special subjects

accomplish. to finish a task

ancient. very long ago or very old

diploma. a document that states a student has finished school

homing instinct. an animal's natural ability to find its way back to its home from a long distance away

landmark. a feature, such as a building, that is well-known and can be seen from far away

magnetic field. the space around a magnet within which the magnet can pull other metallic objects toward it

navigate. to plan how to get somewhere

To see a complete list of SandCastle™ books and other nonfiction titles from ABDO Publishing Company, visit www.abdopublishing.com or contact us at: 4940 Viking Drive, Edina, Minnesota 55435 • 1-800-800-1312 • fax: 1-952-831-1632